2020

To: Emma
A magical story
for a magical you
love
From: Gran Gran
&
Pappa

D1083771

One sunny summer's morning Emma was playing in her garden.

Suddenly she heard sniffling and crying coming from behind a leafy tree.

4

Emma
tiptoed closer and closer
to the whimpering.

When she peeked around the tree
Emma was shocked to see a
little white and purple, sad-looking...

5

UNICORN!

"Hello, my name is Emma,
what's your name and why are you
crying?" she asked the unicorn.

"I'm Sparkle, and I've lost all the magic colours on my rainbow horn from giving out **too many wishes**," said the unicorn.

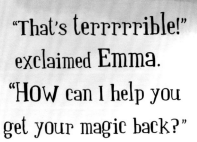

"That's terrrrrible!" exclaimed Emma. "HOW can I help you get your magic back?"

"Well," said Sparkle, "as I become happier colour returns to my horn and when I have all seven COLOURS my magic powers are restored and I can give out wishes again."

Emma had a think, and a wonder and a ponder...

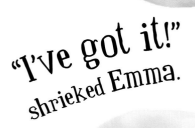

...what could she do?

"I've got it!" shrieked Emma.

"We need to do things that will bring back Sparkle's sparkle!"

#1

SO, they tried playing a game of hide-and-seek.

Sparkle wasn't very good at it but because she enjoyed the game so much the first rainbow colour returned to her horn - ruby RED!

ching!

11

2

Then they sat on squishy
bean bags drinking hot chocolate
and eating rainbow-coloured marshmallows.
This made Sparkle very happy!

slurrrp

With a slurrrp of her hot chocolate,
brilliant ORANGE flashed up on her horn.

"I know what you need
now," said Emma...

"...a PAMPER day!"

So they wrapped up in fluffy robes, had their nails painted, and were so thoroughly **pampered** that sunny

YELLOW

pinged back on to Sparkle's horn.

#3

13

#4

Next up on their fun-filled mission was bouncing UP and dOWn

doing somersaults on Emma's trampoline.

They were having so much fun that Sparkle's emerald GREEN band reappeared on her horn.

#5 Hungry from so much bouncing, the two friends went inside to make unicorn shaped cupcakes.

There was flour and eggs everywhere when the colour sky BLUE appeared on Sparkle's horn.

There were only two more colours to go and Sparkle was feeling so much happier, but what could they do to get the last two?

"AHA!" exclaimed Emma, as she remembered the fun fair had just come to town!

#6

They zipped up and down, whizzed round and round and round on the last loop-the-loop Sparkle squeaked with s...

16

...a bright **INDIGO** band appeared!

...ight...

There was just **one** more colour to go.

7

Exhausted from all the fun the two friends settled down to a **magical film** and some **popcorn**. Sparkle was **so** happy that bold VIOLET, the very **last** rainbow colour, popped back on to her horn.

"That's it! Thank you Emma!" laughed Sparkle. "You have made me so happy that **all** of my magical rainbow COLOURS have reappeared and I can grant wishes again."

"Now, what wish would YOU like?" asked Sparkle. "I wish, wish, wish I could see the Unicorn Kingdom," Emma said hopefully.

19

With a
ZING and a ZAP,
a WHIZZ and a WHIRL,
Emma and Sparkle soared up,
up, up through the
wondrous rainbow.
Then in a flash
of twinkling pink light...

Emma couldn't **believe** her eyes,
she was **really** there and all because she
had helped a **unicorn** have **oodles** of **fun!**

The End

COLOUR
ME IN